CRASH, SPLASH, OR MOO!

For a different Bob,
who sees life as fun

CRASH, SPLASH, OR MOO!

SPLASH

BOB SHEA

LB
Little, Brown and Company
New York • Boston

HOW TO PLAY

Fearless daredevils perform amazing stunts, and YOU guess what happens.

Will they

CRASH?

Will they

SPLASH?

Or will they

MOO?

YAY

Guess right, and win a delicious banana!

Guess ALL the stunts right, and you win the best prize in the world...

Let's meet the team.

ACTION CLAM

First, it's **ACTION CLAM!**
America's favorite splashin', crashin' stunt clam!

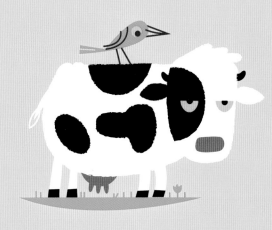

And...this cow!
Who does cow stuff.

And I'm your monkey host,
Mr. McMonkey!
C'mon, let's play!

If **ACTION CLAM…**

drives this **speedy race car...**

into a **giant tower of blocks...**

What do you guess will happen?

Did you guess CRASH?

Give yourself a big round of applause!

You just won your first banana!

clap!

clap!

clap!

clap!

clap!

clap!

clap!

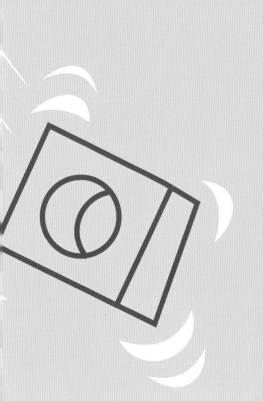

Cow.
A skateboard.

And a super-duper mega-looper!

Okay. For your second banana...
can you guess what **amazing thing**
is about to happen?

Raise your hand if you guess

CRASH!

Raise your hand if you guess

SPLASH!

Raise your hand if you guess

MOO!

(Psst…it's probably not moo.)

Did you guess **MOO?**

Give yourself a big round of applause!

You win
ANOTHER BANANA!

You're a really good guesser!

Okay, Frankie Two-Bananas,
let's see if you can guess
the next one.

STUNT **3**

Action
Clam...

a cannon...

and a really faraway glass of water...

For the next sweet treat you eat with your feet, *what do you guess will happen?*

CRASH

SPLASH

MOO

BOO

CRASH

MOO

Raise your hand if you guess

CRASH!

Raise your hand if you guess

SPLASH!

Raise your hand if you guess

MOO!

*(I'm guessing MOO,
like last time.)*

Did you guess **SPLASH?** Wow!
Give yourself a big round of applause!

You win another banana!

Does that make three? That's plenty to share with a banana-lovin' pal. (Hint, hint.)

3

Only one more stunt until

THE BIG ONE!

Cow...

a motorcycle...

and **TEN** school buses!

Okay, smarty-banana-pants.
What do you guess?

CRASH

SPLASH

Raise your hand if you guess

CRASH!

Raise your hand if you guess

SPLASH!

Raise your hand if you guess

MOO!

(I guess "HONK!")

MO

moo.

MOO????

I did not see that coming!

Did YOU guess MOO?
Give yourself a big round of applause!

You win YET ANOTHER BANANA!
(I'll swing by next week for some banana bread.)

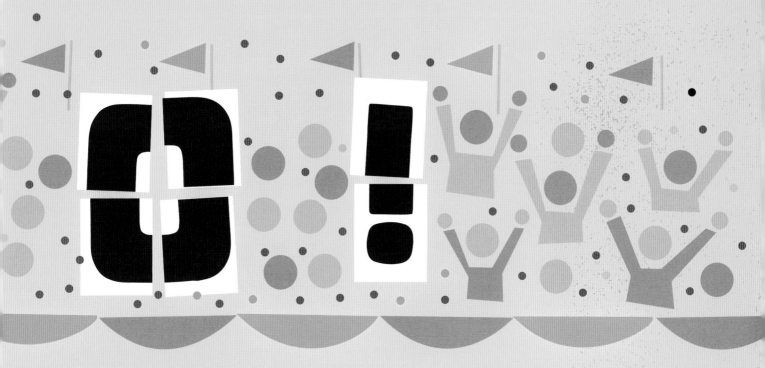

And now, a stunt so big it has an extra-special name.

THE
BiG
ONE

This is for the

MOST SECRET, BEST PRIZE
in the whole wide world.

(No pressure.)

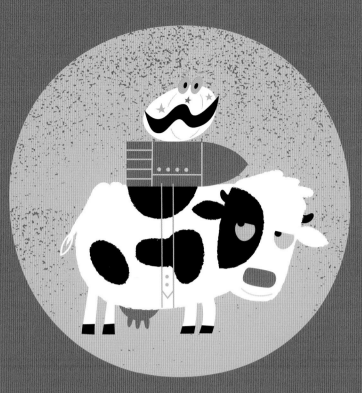

**Action Clam.
Cow.
A rocket pack.**

A piñata.

And a vat of butterscotch pudding.

Raise your hand if you guess **CRASH!**

Raise your hand if you guess **SPLASH!**

WHOOSH!

Raise your hand if you guess MOO!

Raise your foot if I can have a BANANA!

CRASH!

SPLASH!

AND...

Did you guess
CRASH, SPLASH, <u>AND</u> MOO?
Give yourself a big round of applause!

Do you know what else that means?

YOU WIN...

THE WORLD'S

Hold on to your socks,
because they are about to be
KNOCKED OFF!

BEST PRIZE!

THAT'S
RIGHT,
YOU WIN...

Here's a big golden-banana round of applause...
for YOU!

**See you next time for more
stunt-guessing
banana-style action!**

About This Book The illustrations for this book were created digitally. This book was edited by Andrea Spooner and designed by Bob Shea. The production was supervised by Erika Schwartz, and the production editor was Jen Graham. The text was set in Avenir, and the display type is Sol.

Originally published in hardcover and ebook by Little, Brown and Company in: September 2018 • First Trade Paperback Edition: August 2020 • Little, Brown and Company • Hachette Book Group • 1290 Avenue of the Americas, New York, NY 10104 • Visit us at LBYR.com • Little, Brown and Company is a division of Hachette Book Group, Inc. • The Little, Brown name and logo are trademarks of Hachette Book Group, Inc. • The publisher is not responsible for websites (or their content) that are not owned by the publisher. • The Library of Congress has cataloged the hardcover edition as follows: Names: Shea, Bob, author, illustrator. • Title: Crash, splash, or moo! / Bob Shea. • Description: First edition. | New York ; Boston : Little, Brown and Company, 2018. | Summary: Mr. McMonkey hosts a game in which the reader is invited to guess whether a stunt will result in a crash, a splash, or a moo. • Identifiers: LCCN 2018004421 | ISBN 9780316483018 (hardcover) | ISBN 9780316483063 (ebook) | ISBN 9780316482974 (library edition ebook) • Subjects: | CYAC: Guessing games—Fiction. | Animals—Fiction. | Humorous stories. • Classification: LCC PZ7.S53743 Cr 2018 | DDC [E]—dc23 • LC record available at https://lccn.loc.gov/2018004421 • ISBNs: 978-0-316-54106-0 (pbk), 978-0-316-48306-3 (ebook), 978-0-316-48305-6 (ebook), 978-0-316-48304-9 (ebook) • PRINTED IN CHINA • APS • 10 9 8 7 6 5 4 3 2 1